For anyone who needs a reminder of the love we all deserve. The kind that feels like floating amongst stars.

A sky full of stars.
Each one, jealous of you.

CAREFREE BLISS

Sunsets that become sunrises.
Thursdays that become Sundays.

Castles in the sand and laughter in the air.

VOLANS

Love that dives deep and soars high

Portugal

Late night streetlights.
And midnight *bun maska* runs, because
calories don't count with you.

Climbing rooftops on dares.
The city below us, stars above, and
forever ahead.

Dancing in the rain.

And then shivering in pain.

The way your office security guard smiles at me, like he knows our *someday* is just a matter of time.

CORONA BOREALIS

Love that is eternal and true

Greece

The sigh of relief when I spot you in a
crowded room.
The peace you feel when we finally switch
the cocktails for chai, black tie for
pyjamas, and small talk for silence.

When I'm walking with you and you spin me randomly in the middle of the street in a way that has the aunties gasping

My head on your shoulder, and those
forehead kisses you give me when you
really should be watching the road.

*

No plan. No GPS.

SOUTHERN CROSS

Love that guides you home

Polynesia

Pizza that's always cold in a bed that's always warm.

When you write me notes in that scrawly
ant handwriting I pretend not to
understand

Flowers. Lots of them.
So many that the florist near your office started
a college tuition fund for his daughter.

Sweater weather with my hands in
your pockets

DOMESTIC BLISS

The dent in my couch from when it
memorized our tangled feet.

Going back to *our home* instead of
our homes.

Waiting for my '*I'm home*' text
every night before you sleep.
As if I didn't find home
the day I met you.

Your morning chai, exactly the way you like it. No milk. No patience.

All your drawers and sweatshirts that have become *ours*.

The workout you get every time you carry me in.

SUBARU

Love as family, unity, and domestic bliss

Japan

The excitement in your eyes when you serve my parents *chai*. Their polite smiles when they force themselves to drink your crime against humani-tea.

Diwali cleaning = Diwali kissing. I think your maid is still gossiping about the time my kurta may or may not have set your bedroom on fire...

Photos on our wall that make the
neighbors jealous.
"Stunning", they whisper as they see us at
the Taj Mahal and Eiffel Tower and
Wicked Broadway stage. And sure, all that
looks okay.
But *stunning?* That's just for
you.

Your crazy competitive streak whenever
we play Monopoly. And the way you
secretly let my niece win every time

The way you trace the scar on my little finger with a look of disbelief. I told you I'd win our onion cutting race.

PUSHYA

Love that nourishes your soul until it overflows
India

The snacks you sneak into my bag every morning, like I'm going to war instead of office across the street

The pout you give me when you insist that you can carry all our grocery bags. Maybe one day our tomatoes will arrive home unsquished.

Your garden dreams vs. my
plant graveyard.
At least we're optimists?

The way you have tissues ready for everything from our Bollywood binges to national anthems during cricket matches and that Diwali homecoming ad we've seen 50 times. It's okay, I forgive you for not crying at the perfection of the dosa I made for our last Bollywood binge (we both know I ordered in).

Your zombie shuffle to the bathroom
every morning: eyes closed, signature
frown, and tripping over that hoodie you
swore I stole 6 months ago

LAS TRES MARÍAS

Love as protection

Latin America

The look you give me when you spray sunscreen all over me before work, like I have no sense of self preservation. Like keeping me safe is your favorite job.

The way you eat ice cream straight from
the container, while maintaining eye
contact and curving up that corner of
your mouth that smiles just for me.

The way you insert yourself between me and danger: traffic on the road, tofu in my biriyani, and that stare my mother gives me when I refuse to celebrate sexist festivals.

You're my favorite blanket.

My favorite habit.

Resting my head on your shoulder.
You sigh, and I'm home.

PLAYFUL BLISS

The way you sparkle when you steal
mithai from my plate.

LYRA

Love that makes even God bend rules

Greece

That stupid Looney Tunes song you sing in the shower that I definitely didn't record.

Your ridiculous victory dance every time you beat me at WWE on our PlayStation... and the way you let me pin you down after

The way you try to charm my
grandma with your terrible Hindi,
while she pretends to not understand
your English

Your stupid ability to make me laugh
whenever I'm supposed to be mad at you.
No, quoting King Khan with your arms
outstretched does not count as an apology

Your panic face when my little brother swings his cricket bat around and asks about your "intentions"

DELPHINUS

Love as play and laughter

Greece

All those hairstyling videos you watched on YouTube so you could tie my hair when I broke my arm jumping. I promise I'll never jump on our bed when India scores again (I definitely will).

The way you gasp dramatically every time
I suggest we eat dinner before dessert, like
I've personally offended your ancestors.

The way you hide me in your chest whenever we watch horror movies, but claim that *you're* using *me* as a human shield.

Your confidence in the kitchen vs.
my smoke detector's opinion

Your 3-step negotiation tactic: puppy dog eyes, questionable logic, and forehead kisses until I cave.
At least that life size LEGO Batman makes a great coat rack.

Laughter that makes your belly ache.
Hair tucks that make my eyes shine.

When I ask you how I'm looking,
and you tilt your head and say *nice*
while your eyes scream *mine*

All those arguments you won by tickling
me until I surrendered. Cheater,
I hate you.
I couldn't love you more.

INTIMATE BLISS

The smile you designed for me.

CYGNUS

Love as faithful devotion

Slavic Folklore

While our shadows merge on the wall.

Squeezing into your twin size bed in your childhood bedroom. You sleep talking to your teenage self about how you got everything you ever wanted.

Bathing in starlight.

Basking in moonshine.

Tasting your laugh.

SIRIUS

Love as glowing eternity

Egypt

A walk on a hill at 2 a.m. With stars louder than us.

That wink which floods my thoughts with

Later.

All those pictures I take when you're not looking. My favorite mental wallpaper.

That look you give me from the passenger
side that makes us hate seatbelts.

That jacket that smells like you. Draped over my shoulders while you pretend your ears were always that red.

The way you hold my hand tighter when
we face firing squads of nosy aunties and
drunk uncles at weddings

Counting down to New Year's in my ear
instead of with the crowd.

Snowflakes in your hair. Nature's confetti.

PO TOLO

Love that's always shining for you, even when you can't see it
Mali

I don't know if it's fate or destiny or the magic of college admissions and meddling aunties, but every time I look at you... I believe in something.

That second of disbelief on your face every time someone pays you a compliment. It's going to end with me.

The little dimple you get on your thumb when you hold my hand too tight. It's never tight enough.

The way you talk about our kids like
they're already out past curfew.

When you cup my cheeks and say that you're holding your whole world. And the way you hide your smile behind an eyeroll when I ask if that's your way of calling me fat.

HŌKŪLEI

Love as a garland, strung together by cherished bonds
Hawaii

Wandering eyes, colliding thoughts.

That head tilt only I know.

Morning light finds you first.
I'm jealous of the Sun.

My hair, tangled in sunlight.
The map of your freckles, traced in
moonlight.

Someone says your name.
My attention drops everything and runs
straight to them.

Your voice is the most soothing background score to the film of my thoughts.

AL NA'IR

Love as a graceful, lifelong partnership

Arabic Folklore

Every important sentence might start with
me, but always ends with you.
I miss you.
I need you.
I love you.

In every breath. In every lifetime.

Just one more

Kiss

Second

Smile

Hug

Forever

About this Book

I've always loved stars.

There's something magical about looking up to the sky and seeing a beautiful piece of history.

Because every time we see stars, we see them not as they are, but as they were when light left them. Bright, shining, and lighting up our lives, even if they're long gone.

Just like our favorite people... and our best memories with them.

This book is a tribute to those people, moments, and stars. It started as a letter I wrote to myself in the Notes app of my phone during a particularly difficult time, and grew into a reminder of the *I'll cross 7 seas for you* kind of love.

It grew into hope for the love we all deserve.

The one that's blissful.

Simple.

Unconditional.

And forever.

With infinite l⋆ve,
Shriya

About the Stars

in order of appearance

Carefree Bliss

Volans. Portuguese sailors of the 16th century saw flying fish leap beside their ships, and immortalized them in mythology. These fish chased each other through sea and sky, and symbolized the ultimate love: one without limits

Corona Borealis. Greek God Dionysus fell in love with Ariadne, a heartbroken mortal princess. Their love was so radiant that he married her, made her immortal, and placed her crown among the stars, where it shines as the joy of finding your true, eternal love

Southern Cross. Polynesian navigators and Aboriginal Australians used the four stars of the Southern Cross as a compass across vast oceans. These stars showed up in different ancestral stories: always steady, always reliable, and always leading the way home

Domestic Bliss

Subaru. In Japanese, "Subaru" means "to unite" or "come together". The constellation depicts six bright stars gathered close together in the winter sky, creating a family that shines brighter together than any could alone

Pushya. Pushya, one of the 27 lunar mansions, was called the “nourisher” in Indian Vedic astrology. Symbolized by the udder of a cow, it was considered the most auspicious star for beginnings, abundance, and devotion

Las Tres Marías. In Latin America, Las Tres Marías, or the Three Marys, are remembered in tales as sisters or guardians who watched over travelers. They symbolize love that stands watch, protecting you wherever you go

Playful Bliss

Lyra. Greek god Hermes made the first lyre and gave it to Apollo, who passed it to a widower named Orpheus. Orpheus played so beautifully that trees and rivers danced, and even Hades (the Greek God of the Underworld) relented when Orpheus begged for his wife Eurydice's return. After Orpheus's death, the gods placed his harp among the stars as Lyra: love that composes its own symphony, of two hearts strung together

Delphinus. Dolphins were always known as fun and playful creatures. When Greek God Poseidon's wife Amphitrite fled from him, a dolphin acted as a playful messenger and persuaded her to return and accept Poseidon's devotion. For its kindness, Poseidon placed the dolphin in the heavens as Delphinus: a love that unites through joy and play

Intimate Bliss

Cygnus. In Slavic folklore, swans were sacred birds of fidelity, known to mate for life. Cygnus, the swan constellation, was a reminder of their unbroken devotion, flying across the heavens together: love that journeys through every season, never alone

Sirius. Sirius, the brightest star in the sky, is the star of Isis, Egyptian goddess of devotion and marital love. Her loyalty brought Osiris (Isis' brother / husband) back from death, and in her honor, Sirius became a symbol of enduring, life-giving love

Po Tolo. The Dogon people of Mali (West Africa) said the star Sirius had an invisible twin companion, long before science confirmed it. In their cosmology, Po Tolo was a "cosmic twin" of Sirius at the heart of creation itself: love that recognizes its other half, two souls sharing one light

Hōkūlei. Hawaiian navigators named many clusters like Hōkūlei, "star garlands," stringing them into maps that guided voyages across the Pacific. Stars became flowers, woven into the lei of the sky: love that strings moments and cherished bonds together into something beautiful enough to wear forever

Al Na'ir. Al Na'ir means "the bright one" in Arabic. It is part of a crane, which were admired for their grace, elegance, and fidelity, as they were believed to mate for life and migrate together. Arab astronomers saw Al Na'ir as a symbol of faithful partnership and lifelong devotion -- a reflection of beauty, devotion, and loyalty

Thank you for floating through the stars with us

Coming Next
in the Ishq Series

with stars shining for us

ishq #2: firsts

Awaaze is an imprint of Ishq & Insight Studio/Lab founded by Shriya Sekhsaria. Ishq & Insight was created with the mission to bridge the gap between art and science, to understand humanity and to help people build better relationships – including with themselves. Through a combination of books, movies, games, apps, and even psychology experiments, Ishq & Insight hopes to celebrate humanity and spread happiness and love across the world. For more information, please visit or www.ishqandinsight.com

Cover and stars illustrated by Andi Gunawan / Didi Andi

www.ingramcontent.com/pod-product-compliance
Lightning Source LLC
Chambersburg PA
CBHW062111160726
48282CB00026B/754
* 9 7 8 9 3 3 4 4 5 2 0 3 7 *